FARGO PUBLIC

MEET ME ON THE COURT

DAVID ARO

An imprint of Enslow Publishing

WEST 44 BOOKS™

Meet Me on the Court
Nothing But Net
Swish
Fast Break
Big Shots

Please visit our website, www.west44books.com.
For a free color catalog of all our high-quality books,
call toll free 1-800-542-2595 or fax 1-877-542-2596.

Cataloging-in-Publication Data

Names: Aro, David.
Title: Meet me on the court / David Aro.
Description: New York : West 44, 2019. | Series: Alton heights all-stars
Identifiers: ISBN 9781538382110 (pbk.) | ISBN 9781538382127 (library
  bound) | ISBN 9781538383063 (ebook)
Subjects: LCSH: Basketball--Juvenile fiction. | Teamwork (Sports)--
  Juvenile fiction. | Friendship--Juvenile fiction.
Classification: LCC PZ7.A76 Me 2019 | DDC [E]--dc23

First Edition

Published in 2019 by
Enslow Publishing LLC
101 West 23rd Street, Suite #240
New York, NY 10011

Editor: Theresa Emminizer
Designer: Seth Hughes

Photo credits: cover © istockphoto.com/efks

Printed in the United States of America

CPSIA compliance information: Batch #CS18W44: For further information contact
Enslow Publishing LLC, New York, New York at 1-800-542-2595.

CHAPTER ONE

THE WORST NEWS

The day started off great. It was the day after Halloween. The bus driver played the radio on the way to school. And not the oldies she usually played. The pop music the kids actually liked. The boys in the back seats played air drums. The girls sang. Three best friends named Tyler, Cam, and Markus traded their favorite candies.

Tyler liked peanut butter cups. Cam liked suckers. Markus wanted gummy candy.

They each shoved candy in their mouths. Tyler tried to say something. But it didn't work. The peanut butter glued his mouth shut. He wiped the chocolate off his lips.

"I can't believe today is finally here," said Cam.

"I couldn't sleep last night," said Markus.

"Ya sure?" joked Brianna. She and Jasmine sat across the bus aisle. They lived in Alton Heights housing, too. "Your hair looks like you just rolled out of bed."

Markus checked his hair with his hands. "You're one to talk. You look like you just rolled off the court. You know you don't have to wear a wristband *all* the time. Only when you're playing basketball."

Brianna stuck her tongue out at Markus. She pulled the sleeve of her hoodie over her wrist.

"You guys aren't the only ones excited for basketball tryouts today," said Jasmine. She put her backpack over her shoulder.

When they got to school, they all got off the bus together.

The boys played follow the leader to

their classroom. Tyler took a big jump off both his legs. Cam hopped behind him. Markus was the joker of the group. He knocked into Cam's back. The three of them fell into the room. Jasmine picked up a piece of paper from the floor. She shot it into the trash like a basketball. Slam dunk!

"That will be all," said the teacher. Mrs. Avery sat on the edge of her desk with a smile.

Mrs. Avery decorated for every season. Pumpkins still sat in front of the window. But she had taken the ghost cutouts off the walls. Red, orange, and yellow leaves took their place. A giant turkey hung on the bulletin board. Just another clue that it was almost basketball season.

"I have a special surprise," said Mrs. Avery. She tucked her white hair behind her ear.

All twenty kids sat straight up in their seats like bowling pins. Quiet. Hardly moving as they waited.

Mrs. Avery reached around the side of her desk. She pulled a plastic bag from her purse.

The kids couldn't sit still any longer. Cam jumped from his seat. He was so fast he beat everyone to the desk. Jasmine and Brianna laughed. The rest of the class stepped up for a better view. Markus snuck a gummy worm from his pocket. Tyler stood in the back. Being the tallest, he could see over everyone.

Mrs. Avery unwrapped a tablet from the bag.

"I've always wanted one of those!" said Jasmine.

"Do we all get one?" asked Markus.

Mrs. Avery quieted the class with her hands. "We are very lucky to have *one* in our class this year."

"Only one?" asked Cam.

"Now, now," said Mrs. Avery. "There's more to life than things."

The class didn't want another life lesson. Brianna rolled her eyes. Jasmine played with her hair. Markus lowered his head.

Mrs. Avery noticed the sour faces. She pretended to put the tablet back in the bag. "I guess we don't want to take turns using it in our groups this morning."

"No, no!" said Cam.

The class hurried back to their tables. Tyler's group used the tablet first. Cam, Markus, Jasmine, and Brianna huddled in close as Tyler turned it on.

The tablet opened to the Golden Roots Prep homepage. Except that wasn't their school.

"What's wrong with the tablet?" asked Tyler.

Mrs. Avery walked over to the kids' table and took a seat. "Oh. Golden Roots Prep gave some of their extra electronics to our school."

"I heard every student there got a brand-new laptop this year," said Jasmine.

"That must be nice," added Cam.

"They're not any better than you," said Mrs. Avery. She brought up the Center Park Elementary website. Then handed the tablet back to Tyler.

And that's when the day changed for the worse.

"BASKETBALL TRYOUTS CANCELLED." The words were large on the homepage. Tyler clicked on the bright red letters over and over. But they didn't change. Written below them it said, "Due to lack of funding."

Tyler, Cam, Markus, Jasmine, and

Brianna all looked like they had seen a ghost. Everyone knew how much the five of them loved basketball.

Tyler dropped the tablet on the table and raised his hand.

"Yes, Tyler," said Mrs. Avery.

"How could we not have enough money for a basketball team?"

"I'm sorry, guys," Mrs. Avery said. "The school is doing the best that we can."

CHAPTER TWO

AN IDEA IS BORN

The rest of the day dragged on and on. Tyler, Cam, and Markus didn't talk much. They didn't whisper to each other. They didn't raise their hands to answer a question. They mostly stared out the window.

Even Jasmine and Brianna were quiet. They didn't pass notes until after math. And they didn't talk again until lunch.

"I can't believe they cancelled tryouts," said Jasmine.

She took a bite of a carrot.

"I know," said Brianna. "I wish there was something we could do."

Tyler, Cam, and Markus sat alone at the next table over. They looked very unhappy.

Tyler tore the crust from his turkey sandwich. He took only one bite. Cam pulled his sandwich apart. He ate the half with peanut butter on it. Markus finished the last of his gummy worms.

"What are we going to do now?" asked Markus.

"Maybe our parents could do something," said Cam.

But none of their parents knew much about basketball. And no one had money to spare. That was part of why Tyler, Cam, Markus, Jasmine, and Brianna were such close friends. They all lived in the same worn-down housing complex, Alton Heights.

They had all grown up together. They even learned to ride on the same bike. Markus's father had picked it up at a garage sale for only a few bucks. They called it the Green Speedster. Green specks were the only color left on the metal frame.

"No. We'll have to figure this out on our own," said Tyler.

Tyler threw away the rest of his lunch.

Mrs. Avery walked from the lunchroom doors. She met Tyler next to the trash. "Done with your lunch already?"

"Yeah," Tyler sighed.

Mrs. Avery looked at her watch. "Are you sure? Lunch isn't even halfway through."

Tyler shrugged his shoulders.

"I know what might cheer you up," said Mrs. Avery. "Would you like to go to the gym until the bell rings?"

Tyler's eyes widened.

"Really?"

"Yeah. Why not?" answered Mrs. Avery.

Tyler waved over to Cam and Markus.

They threw away their lunches and joined Tyler.

"Just be careful," called out Mrs. Avery.

The three of them skipped down the hall to the empty gym. Cam turned on the lights. They buzzed. The lights were soft at first. Like a flashlight when the power goes out.

Tyler found the only ball in the gym. It hid in the dusty corner under the bleachers. He bounced the ball hard. Dust flew off the ball. The noise sounded across the gym. Then the lights came on full blast.

"Catch." Tyler threw the ball to Markus.

Markus took a shot from half-court and missed.

The three boys forgot about their bad news. They passed the ball back and forth. Tyler dribbled between his legs. Cam dribbled around his back. Markus tried to dribble the ball with his knee.

They played a game of P-I-G. Tyler won.

Cam grabbed the ball. "Ten seconds

left in the game!" he said. He passed the ball to Tyler. Then he ran to the other end of the court. Tyler tossed the ball to him for a layup.

"And he scores!" shouted Markus.

Just then, an idea was born.

"Hey. Why don't we make our own team?" asked Tyler.

"What do you mean?" asked Cam.

Tyler grabbed the ball from Cam. "The three of us. We can keep practicing together." He nailed a shot from the three-point line. "See, it's perfect!"

The bell rang.

"I'm in," said Markus.

"Me, too," said Cam.

They gave each other high fives. It was settled.

CHAPTER THREE

PRACTICE, PRACTICE, PRACTICE

Mrs. Avery made a deal with Tyler, Cam, and Markus.

"Pay attention in class. If you do, I'll let you eat lunch in the gym all week."

The three of them agreed. Every time Mrs. Avery asked a question, Tyler, Cam, and Markus raised their hands.

"How many degrees are in a right angle?" asked Mrs. Avery.

"Ninety," answered Cam.

"What's the chance of a coin landing on heads?"

"That's easy," said Markus. "One out of two. Fifty percent."

"What element has the symbol He?"

Tyler paused. He looked down at the floor. Then up at the ceiling. His forehead wrinkled as he tried to remember. He saw the tablet on the table with the lesson still open. "Helium."

"Very good, Tyler."

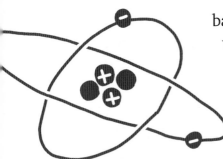

"Isn't that the stuff in balloons that makes your voice sound funny?" asked Markus.

"*You* don't even need that," said Brianna.

Tyler, Cam, and Jasmine laughed.

"Yes, Markus," answered Mrs. Avery.

They did better in class than ever. Mrs. Avery kept her promise.

Tyler, Cam, and Markus ate lunch in the gym. They spent most of the period playing basketball.

Each day, they focused on something new. Tuesday, they practiced layups off the backboard.

Wednesday, they practiced passing, chest passes, and bounce passes. Then they did overhead passes. And of course, behind-the-back passes. Markus didn't have as much luck as Tyler and Cam with those. He kept hitting himself in the back with the ball.

Thursday was for free throws. Tyler shot six in a row. Cam five. Markus three.

Friday, they goofed around. They had trained hard all week.

The boys tried to make a basket by bouncing the ball off the ground. Nobody made it. But Markus did make one trick shot. He punted the ball like a football. It flew right into the hoop! Tyler and Cam cheered.

The week turned out better than the team thought it would. They got to play basketball during lunch *and* Mrs. Avery sent a note home for each of their parents.

She told their parents about their good behavior. The parents decided the kids were grown up enough to walk home from school together.

They only lived about a mile away. And the park between the school and the Alton Heights housing complex had a basketball court.

"You just have to keep up the good work." Tyler's mom kissed him on the forehead after dinner. Then she left for her second job as a cashier.

Every day after school, the three boys ran out of the building. They could have taken the long way. But instead, they cut between the houses behind the school. The straighter the path, the quicker they reached the park.

They hurried through backyards. Cut across driveways. Ducked under a swing set. One house had a white fence they had to walk around. The dog on the other side sounded like a giant wolf. They ran faster.

Each day, they were pretty much the only people at the park. A few kids rode bikes. An older person walked a dog. A mother pushed a baby on the swings.

Tyler, Cam, and Markus found a worn-out basketball next to one of the hoops. It had a slight bump. It bounced weird if it hit the ground just right. It didn't bounce as high as one of the school balls, but it did the job.

Each night, the boys made it home in time for dinner. They did their homework before bed. And the next day they were allowed back to the park.

They always practiced by themselves. Except on Thursday, when Jasmine and Brianna showed up. The five friends took turns playing two on two.

The girls were pretty good. Jasmine was a great defender. She stole the ball from Cam and passed it to Tyler. He knocked down the shot.

Brianna had a nice handle. She dribbled by Markus and hit Cam for a layup.

"You're lucky no one was around to see me blow by you like that," joked Brianna.

Markus pretended one of his shoes had been untied. *That* was what slowed him down.

Tyler, Cam, and Markus jammed their bags into their lockers after Friday's bell. The weekend meant no homework. They took the quick path to the park. But something was different. The park was full of people.

The team sat on a bench to catch their breath. Tyler wiped the sweat from his head on the sleeve of his shirt. Cam fixed one of his short, tight braids. Markus pulled a gummy fish from his pocket. But they only sat for a minute.

Jasmine and Brianna walked over to them.

Jasmine held the worn-out ball against her hip. "I don't think you guys are gonna get much practice in today," she said.

The sound of another basketball bouncing made the boys jump. This ball had a zing to it. When it hit the backboard, it sounded like a gunshot. That could only mean one thing.

"The Golden Roots Prep kids are here?" asked Tyler.

"Yup," answered Brianna. "Apparently, their gym floor is being refinished for their big pep rally. And since they live nearby, they decided to take over the park. Like they own *that* too."

Golden Roots kids took over the court sometimes in the summer. They lived in huge houses. Just a mile from Alton Heights. Their two worlds only collided on the court.

"Again? You've gotta be kidding me," said Cam.

"I wish," said Jasmine. "I think my mom's making chili, though. Do you guys want to walk home with us?"

Tyler pursed his lips. "No thanks. Not today."

The girls took the ball with them. When they were out of sight, Tyler nodded to Cam and Markus. "You guys ready to show them what we got?"

Tyler, Cam, and Markus walked into the park as a team. Side by side. Ready to put all their hard work to use.

CHAPTER FOUR:

FRIENDS ONLY

It looked like Golden Roots Prep had thrown up on the park. Girls in checkered skirts sat on the picnic tables. They put on lip gloss as they talked. Others had snacks on blankets.

Tyler, Cam, and Markus walked toward the basketball court. All eyes shifted in their direction.

The three best friends tried not to notice the stares. It didn't work. Tyler blushed. Markus shoved his hands in his pockets. Cam smiled back and waved. A yellow-haired girl from one table laughed at him.

When Tyler, Cam, and Markus reached

the court, they were shocked. They
watched the boys playing basketball. Their
sneakers were so white. Brand-new. Much
different than Cam's muddy
shoes. Or Tyler's broken laces.
Markus's shoes weren't falling
apart. But he wore two
different-colored socks. One
green. One blue.

"What do you
think you're
doing?" asked
T.J. He was from
Golden Roots
Prep. He thought he was so cool, no one
could call him by his real name. Just T.J.

Tyler stepped onto the edge of the
court. "We're here to play."

"You want to play?" T.J. pointed to the
boys behind him. "With us?"

All the boys on the court laughed like
it was a joke.

Tyler, Cam, and Markus looked at each
other, not sure what to do.

The boys on the court went back to

playing. T.J. passed the ball to his friend Steve. Steve passed it to his friend Jason. He dribbled down the court. A gold chain flopped around his neck.

Tyler wasn't ready to give up. "What's so funny about it?"

T.J. turned to face them again.

"Maybe I didn't speak slow enough for you," said T.J. He sounded out each word. "This. Is. A. Friends. Only. Game."

The kids on the court kept laughing. Steve lifted the collar of his polo so it stood straight up.

"What's that supposed to mean?" asked Cam.

"What's so hard to understand?" asked T.J. "Do you see any of your friends here?" The boys from Golden Roots Prep stood next to T.J. "No. So you can't play."

Cam and Markus backed away.

But Tyler wasn't ready to give in. "What's the matter? Scared you're gonna lose?"

The park went silent. The girls stopped talking. Even a jogger stopped to watch.

The boys from the court stepped closer to Tyler. Cam and Markus hurried back to Tyler's side.

T.J. walked back and forth in front of his friends. He poked Jason with his elbow. "Can you believe this?"

Tyler didn't know if he had just made a big mistake. His hands got sweaty. He wiped them on the bottom of his shirt. He got ready for what might come next. Cam squeezed his right hand into a fist inside his sweatshirt pocket in case a fight broke out.

"You can't possibly be that stupid," said T.J. He looked directly at Tyler. "Don't they teach you math in that school of yours?"

Tyler, Cam, and Markus knew enough to not answer the question.

"A basketball team needs at least five players." T.J. lifted his hand in the air and counted on his fingers. "One. Two. Three. Four. Five." He held his hand out in front of him as if high-fiving the air. "Five."

"And how many of you are there?" T.J. pointed to Tyler. "One." He pointed to Cam.

"Two." He pointed to Markus. "Three." T.J. counted on his fingers again. "One. Two. Three."

T.J. held a hand in the air with five fingers pointed out. The other hand with three. "You're not a real team."

Markus looked down at the ground.

Cam eyed Tyler.

Tyler stared into T.J.'s eyes. "I think you're scared."

"Scared of you?" T.J. laughed so hard his shoulders lifted up and down. "You must be joking!"

"Then prove it," said Tyler. He took a step towards T.J.

"You want to lose that bad, huh?" T.J. fixed the shoulders of his polo. "Fine. We normally scrimmage ourselves at our pep rally. But I doubt our coach will mind if we have a preseason warm-up game instead."

The boys behind T.J. laughed and clapped.

"This is gonna be so much fun," said Steve. He gave T.J. a fist bump with his left hand.

"Oh," said T.J. "That is, if you can find a real team by then. And in case you need a little help. You need two more players." He held out two fingers. "But we'll understand if you don't show."

"We'll be there," said Tyler.

"Good luck. You're gonna need it," said T.J. over his shoulder. The boys from Golden Roots Prep went back to their game.

Tyler, Cam, and Markus walked home. They weren't sure what they had gotten themselves into. Or where they were going to find two more guys for their team.

CHAPTER FIVE

NO WAY

The weekend went by quickly. And Tyler, Cam, and Markus weren't any closer to finding two more players for their team. News of the game had spread throughout school. Kids whispered in the halls on Monday when the boys walked by.

"I can't believe they're taking on Golden Prep kids!"

"What were they thinking?"

By the time the homeroom bell rang, the whole school was buzzing.

When Mrs. Avery took roll call, Cam covered his mouth with a book. He leaned toward Tyler. "What are we going to do?"

"I don't know," answered Tyler.

Mrs. Avery taught a math lesson. Then the class split into groups.

Tyler's table was the last group with the tablet. The lunch bell rang. And the three best friends stayed in their seats. They stared at the screen.

The boys from Golden Roots Prep had posted mean messages all over social media.

Tyler and his weirdo friends don't stand a chance. Don't miss the big game.

2, 4, 6, 8. For the game we cannot wait!

"We're dead," said Markus.

"We'll think of something," said Tyler. "We have to."

Mrs. Avery was sitting at her desk. She pulled out her brown bag. She started eating celery.

"Would you boys like some?" She held out a baggie of veggies for the boys.

"No, thanks," answered Cam.

"I'm fine," said Markus.

"You know, just sitting there isn't going to change anything." Mrs. Avery started grading papers.

Tyler looked up when the tablet battery blinked red. "What do you mean?"

Mrs. Avery capped her pen. "You boys are worried about the game. Aren't you?"

"How do you know—" Tyler stopped himself. Everyone knew.

"I don't understand," said Mrs. Avery. "You three love basketball. You're probably the best players in school. And you've been working so hard. What's the problem?"

"There's only three of us," answered Cam.

"We need to find two more players," said Tyler.

"And no one will want to play," said Markus, "because everyone's scared of T.J."

"I see." Mrs. Avery placed the graded papers in a folder on her desk. She walked over to the shelf near the window. She grabbed a stack of colored paper. She took some markers and tape. She set them on the table. "How do you know if you don't try?"

So Tyler, Cam, and Markus made signs. *Do our school proud. Join our team. Help us win the big game.*

Mrs. Avery let Tyler, Cam, and Markus put up their signs during the first part of recess.

They started in the school's main entrance. They put one on the board near the main office. They hung some along the locker walls. Then in the gym.

It was empty. But none of the boys felt

like playing. It shouldn't be this hard to find two more players.

"Maybe it was a dumb idea to make a team," said Markus under his breath. Tyler and Cam didn't say anything.

They carried the last of the signs to the lunchroom. The first graders eating lunch sounded like a bunch of noisy birds heading south for winter. Luckily, they were too busy talking to notice the boys hanging their signs.

Tyler, Cam, and Markus put up signs along the lunch line wall. Tyler hung the last sign next to the lunchroom doors.

"Think it'll work?" asked Cam.

"I sure hope so," answered Tyler.

They headed outside to the playground.

Jasmine jumped off monkey bars when she saw the boys. Brianna stood up.

"Any luck yet?" asked Brianna.

"Nope," answered Tyler. "We just finished hanging the signs."

Jasmine ran her hand through her hair. "I'm sure you'll find someone."

The three boys leaned against the school. They looked for anyone who might join their team. The girls waited for the boys to say something. When they didn't, Jasmine and Brianna went back to the playground. They watched the boys from the slides.

CHAPTER SIX

The week went by. Nothing. Nobody
wanted to join the team. Those that might
have were too scared.

"I won't be able to make the game,"
said some.

"My parents said I can't," said the
others.

Tyler, Cam, and Markus took the long
way home from school.

"What are we going to do?" asked
Cam.

"There isn't any more time," said
Markus. "We won't be able to show our

faces at the park again. Or at school."

Even Tyler felt lost. "I don't know what to do."

They walked over the grass growing through the cracked sidewalk of the Alton Heights housing complex. They passed between two rusty cars. One of them was missing a tire.

Tyler kicked rocks in the parking lot. They rolled toward Jasmine and Brianna.

"Hey, guys," said Jasmine.

Brianna shot the worn-out basketball against the building. The ball hit inside their made-up backboard. It was just a spot where some bricks formed a square.

"Still no luck?" Jasmine asked. She smiled at Brianna.

"Nope," answered Cam.

"Well," Jasmine dug the toe of her shoe into the ground. "We have an idea."

"Really?" Tyler asked.

"Yeah," answered Brianna.

"Who can join our team?" asked Cam.

Jasmine and Brianna looked at each other. Then Jasmine poked Brianna.

"We could!" said Brianna.

"Girls. On our team. Against Golden Roots Prep?" Markus cleared his ears with his fingers. "Is that what you said?"

"And what of it?" Brianna passed the ball to Markus. It was harder than he expected. It hit him in the stomach.

"What was that for?" asked Markus.

"You already know we can play," said Brianna.

Jasmine put her hands on her hips. "What other choice do you have?"

Tyler scratched his head. "It's a better idea than not showing up."

Markus looked around like he thought they were being pranked.

"What are you scared of then?" asked Brianna.

Cam looked to Tyler.

The three boys didn't have any other choice. They had passed out flyers. Asked the boys in gym class. Nobody else stepped forward. No one.

"Dinner!" Jasmine's mother called through the window.

The two girls waited for an answer.

Tyler cleared his throat. "This might just work."

"So, we're in?" asked Jasmine.

The boys nodded to each other.

"The Alton Heights All-Stars it is," answered Tyler.

Tyler, Cam, Markus, Jasmine, and Brianna huddled up. They put their hands in the middle, one on top of another. They raised their hands to the sky together and shouted. "Go team!"

CHAPTER SEVEN

IN OVER THEIR HEADS

There was no hiding once the Alton Heights All-Stars walked into the Golden Roots Prep gym. Gold and blue filled the bleachers. Students shook gold noisemakers. They were even louder than the warm-up music.

"You're going down," one person said.

"Look. They have girls on their team!" said another.

The Alton Heights All-Stars took a seat on their bench. They stared out at the unfriendly sea of people.

Cam turned to find his younger brother in the stands between his parents. Markus's parents were next to them. So were Brianna's parents and older brother. And

Jasmine's mother. Everyone except Tyler's mom. She had to work.

Only nine friendly faces in a gym packed with enemies. They were the only ones in the crowd that didn't match the blue and gold shiny floor and painted walls.

Tyler wiped the bottom of his shoes with his hand. Jasmine stretched her legs. Markus couldn't stop watching the crowd. Fans yelled in his direction.

"You don't stand a chance."

"You might as well give up now."

Brianna's brother stood and shouted. "You guys can do it!" But the single voice wasn't loud enough to drown out the others.

"Try not to let them get to you," Tyler said to his team.

That was easier said than done.

Jasmine pulled her hair up into a ponytail.

"Don't break a nail," screamed someone from the stands.

Brianna stopped doing her hair. She jumped over the bench towards the stands.

Tyler grabbed her by the shoulder. "Ignore them."

The five huddled in front of their bench.

"We need to do our talking on the court," said Tyler.

They agreed.

Cam took a ball off the rack. Then the lights went out. They flicked on and off. On and off. Like strobe lights.

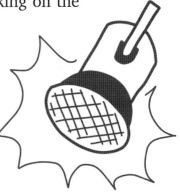

When the lights came back on, gold and blue jerseys circled the court. The whole team wore matching sneakers.

Cheerleaders shook their pom-poms.

The crowd went wild.

The team from Golden Roots Prep formed layup lines. Like they had done it a hundred times.

The Alton Heights All-Stars tried to not let their nerves show. They followed the other team's lead. They started layups on their side of the court. They did okay until Markus dribbled the ball off his foot. Tyler chased down the ball. He called the team back into a huddle near the free throw line.

"I don't know if I can do this," said Markus.

"It's all right, guys," said Tyler. "It's just like the park."

Except it wasn't.

One of the two referees tapped Tyler on his shoulder. "Do you guys have jerseys?"

Tyler looked back at the other team. They looked so official. Unlike the All-Stars in their mismatched T-shirts.

The ref could tell the kids hadn't thought about it. He walked over to the other team's coach. The coach went into the locker room and came out with a brown box. He handed it to the ref.

The ref dropped the box on the floor. "This should do."

Tyler pulled out an old, red, mesh

jersey. The kind kids wear over their T-shirts in gym class.

The Golden Roots Prep team laughed as the All-Stars shyly put them on. Their cheeks turned almost as red as the jerseys.

"Now we're all set," said the ref.

It took a moment for Tyler, Cam, Markus, Jasmine, and Brianna to go back to warming up. By the time they did, they each took only one shot. The buzzer went off.

It was time for the game to start.

CHAPTER EIGHT

GAME TIME

The ref held the ball at center court. He gave it one bounce. Blew his whistle. Tossed the ball in the air.

Tyler won the tip-off. He tapped the ball toward Cam. But Jason stole the ball. He passed it ahead to Steve. Steve passed it to T.J. for a layup. And Golden Roots Prep took an early lead.

Brianna sped the ball up the court. She found Cam open on the wing. He drove past his defender. And hurried a shot. It bounced off the back rim.

Golden Roots Prep slowed the game down. T.J. dribbled the ball with one hand. He held out a finger on the other hand.

Then he called out a play.

Tyler guarded T.J. close. T.J. passed the ball to the right side. Then moved to his left to set a pick on Jasmine. At the same time, Steve snuck up from the block and set a pick on Tyler. T.J. brushed by Tyler for another open layup.

The crowd roared. The All-Stars had played right into the Golden Roots team's plan.

The All-Stars tried to make up for their slow start all at once.

Jasmine took a shot with a hand in her face. Markus lost the ball. Cam jumped into the air with the ball on his way to the hoop. But he didn't have someone to pass it to. He had traveled.

Turnover after turnover, Golden Roots Prep took the lead. They took their time down the court. They ran whatever play their coach called out.

"Two."

"Gold."

"Fist."

Golden Roots Prep took a ten-to-nothing head start.

Tyler called a time-out. It was so loud in the gym, Tyler had to scream for his team to hear him.

"We can still do this. We just have to clean up our plays."

"How do we do that?" asked Brianna.

"We need to take better shots. And talk to each other on defense," said Tyler.

"Yeah," said Cam. "We are better than these guys."

"There's still plenty of time left." Tyler took his hands off his knees. "Let's just take it one play at a time."

They broke out of the huddle.

Brianna passed the ball to Cam. Cam passed it back to Brianna. She hit Jasmine cutting toward the hoop. T.J. helped out on defense to stop her. She found Tyler wide open next to the hoop. Tyler scored the team's first points!

They fought their way back into the game with each possession. They hustled for every rebound. They caught every loose ball. Tyler even jumped out of bounds into the bleachers to save the ball.

By halftime, they were only four points behind.

"See?" said Tyler. "We can do this."

They came out strong in the second half. Brianna had a steal. Cam had four fast-break points. Jasmine knocked down a jumper. And Markus scored after an offensive rebound.

When Golden Roots Prep called time-out, Cam and Brianna each chugged a bottle of water. Markus and Jasmine rested on the bench. And Tyler wiped the sweat from his forehead. The extra effort was tiring the All-Stars out.

Golden Roots Prep wasn't about to give

up. When time-out was over, T.J. scored on a backdoor play.

Neither team could pull away. They traded the lead back and forth. Back and forth.

There was only a minute left in the game. The crowd stood up. They cheered as loudly as they could.

Down one, Brianna crossed half court with the ball. Jason picked off her pass to Markus.

Tyler ran after Jason as hard as he could. The crowd's cheers fueled him faster. He caught up to Jason as he shot a layup. Tyler blocked the ball out of bounds.

Cam gave Tyler a chest bump.

Everyone in the crowd went silent. Except the nine fans not wearing gold and blue. They were cheering loudly. Brianna's brother twirled a towel above his head.

The All-Stars were still down one point. They needed the ball.

Steve inbounded the ball to T.J. Then T.J. dribbled in circles. The clock counted down. Twenty seconds. Nineteen. Eighteen.

Cam, Markus, Jasmine, and Brianna stayed with their Golden Prep players. They blocked T.J. from passing the ball.

The crowd cheered. "Ten! Nine! Eight!"

T.J crossed the ball from his right hand to his left. Tyler went for the ball. He knocked it loose.

The ball bounced to the other side of half court. Tyler picked it up with T.J. on his heels.

The fans shouted, "Four! Three!"

Tyler jumped in the air to shoot. But T.J. grabbed Tyler's arm as the buzzer went off. The ball fell to the floor.

Before the crowd erupted, the ref's whistle blew. "Foul!"

With no time left, the players were taken off the court.

Golden Roots Prep was up by a point. The game rested on Tyler's shoulders. He had two free throws.

He stood alone on the foul line.

The fans behind the hoop jumped up and down. It looked like one giant gold and blue blob. Feet stomped on the bleachers. Noise echoed around the gym.

Tyler wiped his hands on his shorts. The ref bounced him the ball. He took one dribble. Then another. He held a deep breath. Let it out slowly. Then he shot the ball. Just like he had practiced time after time.

The ball bounced off the front rim. It hit the backboard and went in.

Cam, Markus, Jasmine, and Brianna cheered from the sidelines. The game was now tied.

"Don't miss!" yelled Steve. Tyler wiped his right hand on his shorts again. He bounced the ball once. Twice. Took a deep breath.

"Brick!" yelled T.J. from the bench. He

was trying to throw Tyler off. Make him miss the shot. Make him hit the rim again.

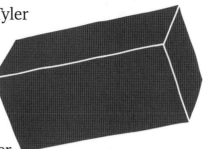

The entire gym was still. Everyone had their eyes on Tyler. Tyler looked up at the basket. He bent his knees, then sprung up. He tossed the ball, following through with his wrist. It flew high in the air.

The ball hit nothing but net. Swish.

Tyler turned to his team. Cam, Markus, Jasmine, and Brianna ran to meet him at half court. They jumped into each other with their arms in the air.

"We did it!" screamed Jasmine.

"We won!" shouted Cam.

Markus did a dance inside his team's huddle. He dribbled an imaginary ball between his legs. Then rolled his shoulders back one at a time.

Brianna joked, "How'd we ever win with this guy on our team?"

"Or with a couple of girls!" Markus

gave Brianna's shoulder a small push.

The five friends put their hands together.

Tyler said, "Looks like the Alton Heights All-Stars are here to stay!"

CHAPTER NINE

RESPECT

Even though their team lost, the Golden Roots Prep fans clapped for the well-played game. Their coach loosened his gold tie under his blue suit. He told his team to keep their chins up. He said, "You played hard."

The Alton Heights All-Stars lined up on the side of the court. They shook hands with T.J., Steve, Jason, and the rest of the Golden Roots Prep team.

Tyler looked at T.J. "Good game," he said.

T.J. said, "You too." He looked at his coach. Then back at Tyler. "Sorry for giving you such a hard time."

"Yeah. You guys aren't half bad," said Jason.

The two teams finished shaking hands.

The Golden Roots Prep team went back to the locker room. The All-Stars walked over to their families.

Cam's father said, "We are so proud of you!"

"You guys were awesome," agreed Brianna's brother. He gave everyone high fives.

Jasmine's mother followed it up with hugs for all five of them.

Markus's father asked, "What do you say we go out for ice cream? My treat."

Tyler's mom got out of work in time to join them at Lil Scoops. She gave Tyler a big hug. "Tell me all about it," she said. A proud-mom tear fell down her cheek.

Then the All-Stars walked back to Alton Heights. With their heads held high.

Want to Keep Reading?

Turn the page for a sneak peek
at the next book in the series.

9781538382134

SPRING PRACTICE

The Alton Heights All-Stars were ready to hit the court.

The cold weather had turned warm. No ice hung from the roofs. The snow had melted on the basketball court.

They could once again wear shorts and sweatshirts outside. To kids at Center Park Elementary, this was a big deal.

It meant the start of spring. And the big kickball game at the park.

The All-Stars split into teams. Tyler, Jasmine, and Brianna ran to the outfield.

Brianna yelled, "You're going down!" Then she pointed to Cam and Markus.

Markus stuck his tongue out at her.

Cam kicked the ball. It flew over Tyler's head. He chased it down. Cam ran around the bases. Tyler kicked it back into play. The ball landed in a puddle next to third base. Mud splashed on Cam's legs.

"Thanks a lot," said Cam. He wiped off his legs with his sleeve.

"Well, next time don't kick it so far!" yelled Tyler from the outfield.

They smiled at each other.

"Easy out. Easy out," called Brianna. She moved toward second base.

Markus rubbed his hands together. He waited for the ball to roll to him. He kicked it over Brianna's head. She ran for it. Then dived. She slid across the muddy grass. She pushed herself up.

"That's the third out," she said. She wiped the mud off her face.

Markus walked by Brianna when they switched sides. "Looks like you missed a spot," he said.

Brianna wiped her hand off on Markus's shirt. "Thanks," she laughed.

ABOUT THE AUTHOR

David Aro is a former Collegiate All-American basketball player and conference player of the year. In college, he scored over 1,900 points, broke his school's record for the most three-pointers ever made, and also finished in the top 10 in rebounds, steals, and assists. While coaching college basketball, he earned a master's degree in executive leadership and change. Today, he coaches his kids and follows his passion of writing children's books. You can visit him online at www.davidaro.com.

Check out more books at:

www.west44books.com

An imprint of Enslow Publishing

WEST 44 BOOKS™